PEANUTS
It's Hockey Time, Franklin!

By Charles M. Schulz

Adapted by Jason Cooper

Illustrated by Scott Jeralds

SIMON SPOTLIGHT

New York   London   Toronto   Sydney   New Delhi

SIMON SPOTLIGHT
An imprint of Simon & Schuster Children's Publishing Division
1230 Avenue of the Americas, New York, New York 10020
First Simon Spotlight edition August 2017
© 2017 Peanuts Worldwide LLC
All rights reserved, including the right of reproduction in whole or in part in any form.
SIMON SPOTLIGHT and colophon are registered trademarks of Simon & Schuster, Inc.
For information about special discounts for bulk purchases, please contact Simon & Schuster
Special Sales at 1-866-506-1949 or business@simonandschuster.com.
Manufactured in the United States of America 0717 LAK
10 9 8 7 6 5 4 3 2 1
ISBN 978-1-4814-8011-6
ISBN 978-1-4814-8012-3 (eBook)

When it's cold outside and the pond is frozen solid, Franklin loves playing hockey with his pal Charlie Brown.

"Hockey is my favorite sport!" Franklin says. "But I also love baseball and football."

"What about Ping-Pong?" Charlie Brown asks.

At the pond Franklin races out onto the ice. Charlie Brown follows but slips and slides across the ice. That's when he notices their friend Peppermint Patty. She is practicing her new figure skating routine.

"Can we share the ice?" Franklin asks. "It's hockey time!"

"Sorry, Franklin," Peppermint Patty responds, "but I'm practicing for the skating show."

"Isn't there room for all of us?" Charlie Brown asks.

"Sorry, Chuck, but I need a lot of space for my figure eights!" Peppermint Patty says.

Franklin and Charlie Brown walk sadly off the ice. "I was really looking forward to playing hockey today," Franklin says.

"I'm not sure if we can play hockey," says Charlie Brown, "but I know where we can watch it." He leads Franklin to Woodstock's birdbath.

Snoopy and Woodstock are standing atop the frozen water, facing off at the puck to start the game.

Franklin stares at them for a moment. "You live in a weird neighborhood, Charlie Brown," he says.

"You know what's weird? Watching a beagle howl the national anthem!" says Lucy.

The boys turn to see their friend Lucy. She's watching the game too. Franklin and Charlie Brown sit in front of her.

"Hey!" Lucy yells. "How did you get better seats than me?!"

Snoopy and Woodstock really get into the game. They play so hard, they break the birdbath and crash to the ground! *Yikes*, Snoopy thinks. *Next time we better wear pads!*

After the game Franklin and Charlie Brown walk back to the pond hoping they can finally play hockey. Snoopy, Woodstock, and Lucy come along too. . . .

Franklin admits, "You know, I had my doubts when I saw the birdbath, but that was the most exciting hockey game I've ever seen!"

Peppermint Patty's friend Marcie is visiting her at the pond. Marcie doesn't skate, so she is cheering for Patty safely from the snow.

"Smooth skating on that figure eight, sir!" she says to Peppermint Patty.

"Thanks, Marcie! But that was actually a figure twenty-seven!" Peppermint Patty responds.

Before Peppermint Patty can start her next maneuver, a group of older kids skate onto the ice and get in her way.

"Move it! I have to practice," Peppermint Patty says to the newcomers.

The older kids just laugh at her.

"We're not moving!" one of the older kids tells Peppermint Patty. "We're here to play hockey! There are ten of us and one of you, so get off the ice!"

Peppermint Patty looks at the kids angrily.

Marcie sees what's happening and bravely charges onto the ice to help. "Don't let them push you around, sir! I'll help you!" Marcie is even worse at running on ice than she is at skating on it. She slips and falls.

"Oh great!" one of the kids says. "How are we supposed to play with this klutz in the way?"

Peppermint Patty has had it. "All right, you jokers! Stop being rude! It's unsportsmanlike!"

Franklin gets his gear on and skates out onto the ice. "What's going on here?" Franklin asks.

"We're fighting for control of the ice! Ten against one!" Peppermint Patty shouts.

"Don't forget me, sir!" Marcie adds. "Ten against *two*!"

Franklin has an idea. "How about we play for control of the ice?" he says to the older kids. "If you win, you get the pond to yourselves. If Peppermint Patty wins, you share the ice."

"A hockey game?" one of the kids asks. "Sounds good to us!"

"Good going, Franklin," Peppermint Patty complains.
"I don't have a hockey team!"
Franklin smiles. "You do now!" he says.

Franklin looks to his friends. "What do you say? Are you ready to play a game? That's what we came here for, right?"
"I came here to figure skate," answers Peppermint Patty, "but now I'm in the mood to defeat those rascally rivals!"
"Nice alliteration, sir!" Marcie declares.

Charlie Brown helps Marcie off the ice. "Thank you, Charles . . ."

Franklin and Peppermint Patty get their team into position.

Lucy is very excited, even though she is facing the wrong direction. "I love hockey ball!" she shouts.

Franklin chooses Snoopy to be goalie. Snoopy puts on extra hockey pads.

"It's not how I imagined, but at least we *finally* get to play hockey!" announces Franklin.

"Not yet," says Peppermint Patty, motioning to Woodstock, who is resurfacing the ice with a tiny Zamboni.

When Woodstock is done, he carries the puck to the center of the ice where Peppermint Patty and the leader of the rival team are ready to face off. "You are going down!" the rival taunts.

Peppermint Patty responds by putting on her game face.

Charlie Brown whispers to Franklin, "In my neighborhood I'm not really known for winning games."
Franklin smiles and says, "Well, in my neighborhood, I am!"

The puck hits the ice, and Peppermint Patty snags it with her hockey stick. Franklin joins her, and they charge toward the goal. Game on!

Patty skates circles around the other players. She passes the puck to Franklin, and he slaps it into the goal!

"Nice shot, Franklin!" Peppermint Patty shouts.

"Okay, this is getting embarrassing!" the rival center shouts. "Let's go play football at my house, guys!"

"So you're giving up already?" Franklin asks.

"We don't give up," the angry center snarls. "We forfeit!"

The rival team skates off the ice.

"Thanks for your help, Franklin," Peppermint Patty says. "I owe you one."

"Don't mention it," Franklin says. "But I do have one request. Can we please play hockey now?"

"Sure!" Peppermint Patty says.

"Hold on," Charlie Brown interrupts. "Here comes the Zamboni again."

Franklin rolls his eyes. "Oh, good grief!"